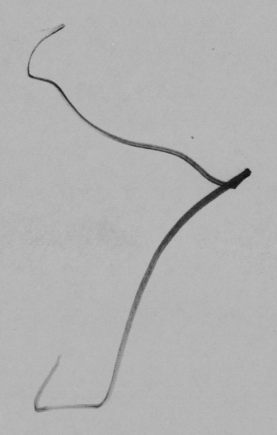

Walt Disney's

Bambi's Forest

A YEAR IN THE LIFE OF THE FOREST

Joanne Ryder

ILLUSTRATED BY *David Pacheco and Jesse Clay*

Disney
PRESS

NEW YORK

First Edition
1 3 5 7 9 10 8 6 4 2

Library of Congress Catalog Card Number: 93-72551
ISBN: 1-56282-643-3/1-56282-698-0 (lib. bdg.)

Walt Disney's

Bambi's Forest

A YEAR IN THE LIFE OF THE FOREST

It is spring in the forest. Near and far, above a young fawn's head, new, perfect leaves dance in the gentle wind. Tall trees, some hundreds of years old, glisten as the rain patters against their needles, leaves, and branches.

As the forest is reborn, patches of green sprout here and there and everywhere. Short, slender spikes of grass peek through the forest floor, and new, soft leaves decorate the bushes and shrubs.

The trees and bushes, grasses and flowers welcome the warm spring rains. Their roots absorb the water so all the woodland plants can grow.

Cold streams, fed by melting ice and snow from the mountains, race through the forest and fill the beaver's pond. Roaring waterfalls tumble grandly from the ragged cliffs of rock. The forest flourishes in the abundance of water.

When the sun breaks through the clouds, the forest is speckled with brightness. Long beams of light stream through the treetops, warming the ground far below.

A young rabbit wiggles his nose, enjoying the fresh, good scent of damp earth heated by the sun.

Delicate blossoms sprinkle the sunniest places within the forest. The fawn chases a butterfly newly emerged from its chrysalis, bobbing among the bright blossoms and drinking their sweet nectar.

Sniffing the fragrant flowers for the first time, the fawn is startled as they stir and part. A young skunk peeks up, curious to see the fawn and this new, bright world, too.

As spring drifts into summer, the skunk and the fawn and the rabbit join other forest young ones growing in size and strength and wonder. Curious and playful, they test their limits whenever they can—dashing faster down the leafy slopes and leaping higher over fallen logs.

Small hoofprints and pawprints mark the forest as the young animals explore new paths—sniffing and listening and looking with care. Each day brings them fresh discoveries and longer journeys through the forest.

Towering trunks stretch skyward, and a canopy of branches forms the forest's leafy roof. Those who fly or climb claim the highest spots in the forest for their homes.

Flickering through the trees, birds sing, announcing their territories. Many have traveled far to nest here during the mild months of spring and summer.

The floor of the forest is covered with a brown carpet of old leaves. They crunch softly underfoot as the fawn and his mother make their way to a shady thicket where they will rest from the heat of a summer's day.

Within the forest, there are clearings of grass and flowers. Grass grows high in the meadow, free from the shade of the old trees. It is home to ground-dwelling birds and seed-eating mice.

At dawn and dusk, when the meadow is cool, misty, and safe, forest creatures come searching for food.

Rabbits carefully leap here and there, then stop to nibble the meadow's leaves and blossoms. They share this meadow morning with the deer, grazing and running in the lush, open space.

By summer's end the forest is rich with berries, nuts, fruits, and seeds. Seeds from grasses and plants fly through the air, landing wherever the wind takes them.

As the nuts and fruits ripen, squirrels and birds perch on the branches, eating their fill. The rest fall to the ground to sprout and grow, to be gathered or eaten.

Under a large oak tree, the fawn tastes his first acorns and looks for more to eat. The tree may yield several thousand acorns now. Few will grow into trees. Most will be eaten or stored for the long winter ahead.

The forest changes as the temperature drops lower. Many trees will rest until the mild weather returns.

The perfect leaves of spring and summer have grown old and worn, battered by storms and nibbled by insects. Each tree turns its own shade of autumn. Yellow birches, red and orange maples, and brown and red oaks fill the forest.

First a few bright leaves, then many, drift from the branches and twigs to speckle the streams and carpet the forest in glowing hues.

Many bushes also turn brilliant, then bare. After the last fall flowers bloom, their petals drift down, too. The first frosts cast a sleeping spell on the resting woods.

Up through the branches, wings flutter as birds and butter-
flies soar away from the forest. Their journey will take
them to warmer forests and fields richer in food.

Down through the soil, claws dig as animals burrow,
seeking resting places to spend the cold days.

While others hide, the young skunk, grown fat, digs
and searches for insects underground.

A hush falls over the forest when the chilly weather turns bitter. The ground lies hard and frozen, and the pond is covered with ice. Mute and motionless, the waterfall is frozen against the cliffs of rock.

Gray skies cover the gray forest, and freezing rain stiffens as icicles on the branches. Few wander through the forest now except to find food or better shelter.

One day snow blankets the ground and paints the forest white.

The deer have grown heavier coats of fur for protection against the cold. They stay in a smaller area of the forest now, making their own paths in the deep snow and eating whatever twigs and buds they can find.

Through the harshest days, a skunk sleeps, unharmed by winter's icy touch.

Slowly at first, the sun begins to thaw ice and snow and frozen ground. Gently, signs of rebirth appear in the forest.

The first shoots of green grass peek from the wet meadow, and the first bird finds his favorite tree in the woods and sings from his old perch.

A rabbit, one year old and warmed by the sun, leaps easily over logs covered in new green moss.

Wandering from his winter resting place, a skunk finds the first small patch of flowers blooming once more.

A young buck walks gracefully through the green forest. Like the trees stretching high, he is stronger and taller than before. His first pair of antlers is starting to grow.

The buck sniffs the familiar scent of warm earth and feels the ground soft under his hooves once more. The forest is green and growing again.